MCP Books
2301 Lucien Way #415
Maitland, FL 32751
407.339.4217
www.millcitypress.net

© 2019 by Christy Zwenger

Printed in the United States of America

ISBN-13: 978-1-5456-72716

LCCN: 2019-908683

No more learning of it in school.

No more signing your name with your signature.

No more penmanship.

Done!

Finished!

CURSIVE WRITING
IS BEING TAKEN AWAY!

"I can't believe it!" shouted letter X, the big mouth of the bunch.

He's that way because he's hardly ever seen in words!

Letter **Q**, barely used as well, and more ladylike, questioned:

"Don't they realize that without us, writing becomes a more tedious task? When you print, you have to pick up your pencil each time you form a new letter. Your hands get tired more quickly! With us **CURSIVE** letters joined together, we make it easy, fun —and pretty too!"

"And people don't realize how writing with us, is so brain enriching!" added Letter **E**, the most educated of the crew.

"Why are they doing this to us?" blubbered

lowercase **i**, the baby of the bunch.

"What would the writers of our United States Constitution say about this? We helped them back then!" shouted capital S.

Letter F fumed with fury!

Letter H threw one big hissy fit!

Letter M even mumbled a few words that need not be repeated!

The **Wisest** one of the pack, letter **W**, spoke up. "Cursive Letters, we have been silent way too long. Our patience and kindness has ended. It is high time, I believe, for us Cursives to

REVOLT!!"

"Revolt?" the crowd squawked!

"Our game plan is really quite simple. All we do is kidnap everybody's penmanship. **How,** you may ask? We, my **CURSIVE** comrades, will disappear!"

"What? How can we do that? How can we become invisible? HOW?"

The **CURSIVE** foursome roared!

F and **T** couldn't handle the shock, each being a bit top-heavy, and fainted under the pressure of this ghastly idea!

W proceeded: "Cursive Letters! Keep your wits about you! Listen! M's cousin, Martin, owns a magic shop. He has disappearing dust that works like a charm. We get doused with it, and poof, we disappear. All Cursives on the planet evaporate! While we are out of sight, we won't be out of mind!"

"Can you see it? The world will be **begging** us to come back. It's the perfect plan. Are we **united** in this?"

The excited letters agreed with high fives and thumbs up.

Magic Martin arrived in no time, commanding the group to huddle together as he drenched **THE CURSIVES** with a **super-duper** dose of his **disappearing** dust.

"The magic lasts exactly **24 HOURS**," sputtered Martin. "I sure hope you get what you want out of this," and off he went.

As morning awakened, each cursive vanished into nothingness.

"I feel so light," mumbled Cursive L.

"Our tails are disappearing!" gurgled lowercase g, p, j, and y.

Soon to be invisible, the letters awaited the day's adventures.

Meanwhile at the Oval Office, Mr. President felt the change in the air. "Hmmmm, something isn't right here," he muttered, as he grabbed his morning brew.

Morning papers were being opened everywhere with only half the news. No one could read their paper completely.
The CURSIVE LETTERS were missing!

As school bells rang, the **calamity** continued. Not a single student could write their name, or even a paragraph for that matter.

The **CURSIVE LETTERS** were missing!

Post offices around the world were in a dither! Half the mail could not be delivered. Envelopes were blank! Post cards were naked!

The CURSIVE LETTERS were missing!

Teachers were tearful. They couldn't sign their report cards! The CURSIVE LETTERS were missing!

Doctors were in a dilemma.

They couldn't sign their prescriptions!

The CURSIVE LETTERS were missing!

Bankers boo-hooed. They couldn't sign their contracts!

The CURSIVE LETTERS were missing!

By NOON, all offices had closed for the day.

No business.

No signatures!

No CURSIVE LETTERS!

Back at the Oval Office, Mr. President had his own predicament percolating!

He was scheduled to sign the treaty that would end the "War of Wars," and his signature was needed by midnight!

HOLY CATS!

As the clock struck 11:00, **THE CURSIVES** were still under the magic, which would last until morning. What could be done? Who could help?

In a flash, Magic Martin was summoned. "Forgive us, but we need to come back earlier than expected," begged THE CURSIVES. "The president is in a BIG PICKLE and needs our help!

World peace depends on us! Please change us back NOW!"

Martin shuffled through his magic mix until he found his

"Quick as a Wink Reappearing Ink."

Just a few drops and . . . PRESTO!

The **CURSIVES** were brought back just in time! The president signed the truce and **PEACE** reigned throughout the world! And with the **PEACE**, the **CURSIVE HEROES** too!

Stay tuned for more adventures with THE CURSIVES!

CHRISTY GAY ZWENGER is an accomplished writer and educator and ... lover of Life! With a Master's Degree in Education and 30+ years of classroom teaching, she has much to say about the Cursive Letters and their importance to Society.

Read more at www.christyzwenger.com.

Christy lives at the ocean with her husband and spends summers on Lake Michigan. Her inspiration comes while swimming in big blue water; reading a "can't put down" book; and writing on topics she's passionate about!

Christy encourages: "Be true to yourself ... LIVE LIFE FUN ... and ... master the art of Cursive!"

Find her classes on cursive on YouTube.

Visit **THE CURSIVES** at www.thecursivelettersrevolt.com.

STEVE RADZI was born Stefan Radziwillowicz in Devon, England, of Polish parents. He is a commercial illustrator by trade, with more then 25 years experience in special event rendering, storyboard art, animation, and set design.

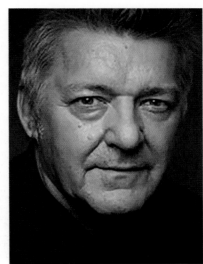

He has traveled extensively and has spent time in Morocco, India, and the Far East. Steve also worked for Hanna-Barbera and designed the orginal pre-production drawings for the animated feature film, "The Hobbit." In addition, Steve hosted his own Reggae radio program on WDNA.FM Miami for 20 years.

With a passion for Maya archaeology and culture, Steve has spent many years traversing, documenting, and illustrating the Maya sites of Mesoamerica. His work may be viewed at www.mayavision.com.

His unique creativity with attention to detail has truly brought the